DATE DUE

Hank THE Pet Sitter

#4
Elmer the Very Sneaky Sheep

by **Claudia Harrington** illustrated by **Anoosha Syed**

Calico Kid

An Imprint of Magic Wagon
abdopublishing.com

Special thanks to Marie Parent & Streaker, the original Elmer —CH

For Mirha —AS

abdopublishing.com

Published by Magic Wagon, a division of ABDO, PO Box 398166, Minneapolis, Minnesota 55439. Copyright © 2017 by Abdo Consulting Group, Inc. International copyrights reserved in all countries. No part of this book may be reproduced in any form without written permission from the publisher. Calico Kid™ is a trademark and logo of Magic Wagon.

Printed in the United States of America, North Mankato, Minnesota.
092016
012017

Written by Claudia Harrington
Illustrated by Anoosha Syed
Edited by Heidi M.D. Elston
Art Directed by Candice Keimig

Publisher's Cataloging in Publication Data

Names: Harrington, Claudia, author. | Syed, Anoosha, illustrator.
Title: Elmer the very sneaky sheep / by Claudia Harrington ; illustrated by Anoosha Syed.
Description: Minneapolis, MN : Magic Wagon, 2017. | Series: Hank the pet sitter ; Book 4
Summary: Hank pet sits Elmer the very sneaky sheep. Elmer can open doors and escape.
Identifiers: LCCN 2016947636 | ISBN 9781624021909 (lib. bdg.) | ISBN 9781624022500 (ebook) | ISBN 9781624022807 (Read-to-me ebook)
Subjects: LCSH: Sheep--Juvenile fiction. | Pet sitting--Juvenile fiction. | Pets--Juvenile fiction.
Classification: DDC [E]--dc23
LC record available at http://lccn.loc.gov/2016947636

Table of Contents

Chapter #1
The New Kid

It was summer, and Hank was bored. His bike was still broken. His friends were still gone. Only Janie was home.

Janie was bossy. Janie was annoying. Janie was right there. Again.

Hank hoped he'd get a new pet to sit. Soon.

He plopped in the dirt and dug for worms.

"Worms are good for the soil, you know," said Janie.

"Don't you have a lawn to mow?" asked Hank.

"If worms don't have food, water, and the right temperature, they'll leave," said Janie.

"You don't have food or water," said Hank. "Why don't you leave?"

"Tsk," said Janie.

Tsk!

"Hi," said a kid. Hank had never seen him before. "Do you know where Hank lives?"

"Who's asking?" Janie pulled a camera from her purse and snapped the kid's picture. "You can't be too careful, you know."

"Don't mind her," said Hank. "I'm Hank."

"Great," said the kid. "I hear you pet sit."

"Yes!" said Hank.

9

The kid kicked the dirt. "I'm Tommy. We just moved in. Our sheep sometimes escapes. Can he stay in your garage? It's just for tonight."

"How does he get out?" asked Hank.

Tommy grinned. "He opens doors."

Hank's eyes bulged.

"But he'll be fine," said Tommy. "Our goat and duck won't be here to egg him on."

"Tsk," said Janie. "I don't like the sound of that."

"Who asked you?" said Hank. "I guess it's okay."

"Great!" said Tommy. "I'll be right back."

Chapter #2
Meet Elmer

Tommy returned, pulling a wagon brimming with hay. Behind him trotted a fat sheep. "This is Elmer."

"Hi," said Hank.

Baaaaaa, said Elmer.

BAAAA!

"He likes to lie on fluffy pine shavings," said Tommy. "And here's some hay and clover, in case you don't want him eating your yard. He'll follow you for fruit or animal crackers."

"Yum," said Hank.

Baaaaaa, said Elmer.

"See you tomorrow," said Tommy. "Then maybe you can come over and swim. We have a pond."

"Cool," said Hank.

Tommy turned to go. "And Elmer's housebroken. So don't worry if he shows up inside. Bye!"

Inside! What had Hank gotten himself into?

Chapter #3
Back to Bed

That night, Hank snuggled under his bedcovers. It sure was weird having a sheep in the garage.

The house was dark. The house was quiet.

Except for that *clomp-clomp*.

Was it a burglar? Was it a ghost?

Hank scooted down lower. He pulled the covers over his head.

Baaaa, said Elmer.

Hank peeked out. "Elmer? Go back
to bed!"

Baaaaaa, said Elmer. He was so
close, they could touch noses.

Hank bribed him to the garage with
a banana. He fluffed his shavings.
"Just the way you like it!"

When Hank got under his covers
again, he nodded right off.

Baaaa, said Elmer.

"Don't you sleep?" asked Hank.
"How about a bedtime story? Then
back to bed. I mean it!"

Hank read about the big, bad wolf.
Elmer just stood there.

"Too scary?" asked Hank. "How about some water? Then back to bed, Elmer."

Hank poured water for Elmer. He poured hot cocoa for himself, with four marshmallows.

Elmer sniffed the air. He nosed Hank's mug.

CRASH! Cocoa splattered all over.

"Hank?" called his mom.

"I'm okay," Hank answered.

"Uh-oh," said Hank. Chocolate dripped from everywhere. Elmer's coat was gooey with marshmallow.

"How about a nice bath?" whispered Hank. "Then back to bed, Elmer."

Hank yawned. He ran Elmer a bubble bath. He used LOTS of bubbles.

"Uh-oh," said Hank. "Did you let your friends in?"

A duck splashed suds everywhere. A goat nibbled toilet paper. What would his mom do if she saw this?

"Let's clean up this mess," whispered Hank. "Then back to bed."

Baaaaa, said Elmer.

Chapter #4
ZZZZZ

Hank dried Elmer with his mom's hair dryer. Elmer got so big, he looked inflated! What would Tommy say?

Janie poked her head in the window. "What's all the noise? My parents said I could investigate."

"Elmer is too poofy," said Hank. "I don't think he'll fit through the door."

"I'll be right in," said Janie. She pulled scrunchies from her purse. "He looks adorable in pigtails!"

Hank shook his head. "He looks ridiculous. And he still won't fit. Go home. I have an idea."

When Janie left, Hank aimed the goat at Elmer and gave him a nudge. But the goat spotted Hank's mom's robe on a hook. He nibbled the belt.

"Oh no," said Hank. He ran to the kitchen for animal crackers.

"Back to bed, everybody," said Hank. He dropped the animal crackers one by one, leading them all out to the garage.

Hank fluffed Elmer's shavings. Then, he tiptoed back to bed and closed his eyes.

But it was too quiet. Hank couldn't sleep.

He snuck to the garage and curled up in the straw. The duck perched on Hank's feet. The goat chewed in his sleep. Elmer snuggled close.

Baaaaaa, said Elmer.

But Hank didn't hear him. He was fast asleep.

When Tommy came the next day, Hank wasn't in his yard. He wasn't in his kitchen. He wasn't in his room.

"Elmer?" called Tommy. He tiptoed into the garage.

Janie twisted Elmer's coat into sparkle clips. The goat nibbled Elmer's hay. The duck flapped from the rafters. And Hank snored in his sleep.

"Awesome, Hank," said Tommy. "They sure like you! Come over when you wake up." He slipped money in Hank's jar. Then he led Elmer and his friends back home.

Bike Money